Arley

Devil's Advocates, Volume 5

S L Davies

Published by S L Davies, 2022.

ARLEY

First edition. September 13, 2022.

Copyright © 2022 S L Davies.

ISBN: 979-8215939413

Written by S L Davies.

Prologue

Flynn

"Arley has been asking about you," Harry said with a smirk as I sat on the edge of his desk.

I rolled my eyes. Harry hasn't stopped talking about him since meeting the Devil's Advocate at my best friend Dylan's home. I admit that I am very intrigued by the vampire. And the thought of having him fuck me every which way but Sunday really is pleasant. But I don't play like that. I know my heart, and I know damned well if I give myself over to one night of pleasure, I'll fall in love and then break my heart.

It was the reason I held Harry back. I knew that he was meant to be mine. Every time I was around the bear shifter, my unicorn cried out to finally mate. But until Harry was willing to make me his, I wasn't about to just play. I wasn't going to have my heart broken. Well, not again.

I didn't talk much about my life. Dylan knew a little bit, but I'd kept my past a secret for the most part. I wasn't necessarily ashamed of where I'd come from; I just didn't want to think about it. My past hurt.

I grew up with my mother, Matia. My father was just a one-night stand. Mama did her best, but she struggled with alcohol. It was her demon, and she couldn't let it go. I tried hard to keep her sober, but it wasn't enough to hold her away from the bottle. She would get sober for a few months and inevitably fall off the wagon. I'd come home from school expecting to find the baked cookies or cupcakes that I'd gotten used to, only to find her on the floor surrounded by a sea of vomit.

There was a constant wave of stepdaddies in and out of my life. If I was really unlucky, some random guy would be passed out on the couch with his dick hanging out from the fuck session they'd not long finished. As I got older and started to work, I tried to encourage Mama into rehab and get her sober. After a few months, she'd be back on the booze again.

It was a vicious cycle that I thought was never going to end. And then I met Luke. He was a fae that my mother had brought home from the pub. I was nineteen and had just come home from a shift at the supermarket where I'd managed to land a job. Mama was passed out on the floor. She was naked, and her clothes were strewn about everywhere. Vomit stretched around her head like a halo.

Luke was sitting on the couch, rolling a cigarette. He wasn't like the other men that Mama brought home. Usually, they would be fat pigs that stunk. Luke was handsome. His body was trim but taught. His red hair was a riot of curls, while his green eyes shone with a clearness that told me he wasn't drunk or a junkie.

"Hey man, I'm Luke. This your Ma?" he asked with a strong English accent.

I nodded and glanced down at my mother, who looked like she'd been through the wringer. Her pale skin was greying, and I wondered how much she'd had to drink.

"Found her wandering down the street, naked as a jay bird," he said with a sigh. "She was able to tell me where she lived, but she vomited and collapsed on the floor as soon as I got her inside. I saw your photos on the wall, so I hoped that you still lived here to check on her when you got in. Thought I'd stick around to make sure she was alright."

I looked back at Luke with a frown on my face. "Thanks," I mumbled. "Were you just outside?"

Luke chuckled and nodded his head. "Yeah, I was going for a jog. Just moved in a few houses up."

I nodded again, not sure whether to be completely mortified. No, scratch that, I was utterly mortified. After that day, Luke and I became fast friends, and eventually, it crossed the line, and we found ourselves in love. I wanted him to mate with me. He held off. I never understood why.

It was my twentieth birthday when I did the pregnancy test to discover I was pregnant. I was thrilled. I couldn't wait to be a Papa. I would give my child a life that I never got. I'd gone home filled with excitement. I couldn't wait to share the news. What I never expected was to see him buried in my mother.

I'd walked into the living room and heard my mother in the throes of passion while she bounced on top of my partner, the father of my child. Luke had looked at me with a smirk on his lips as I turned wordlessly and left the room. My stomach was filled with nausea. I couldn't bear the thought of the betrayal. I questioned everything. *Had this been going on the entire time?* I packed my belongings and left. I didn't even leave a note. I was so angry but destroyed at the same time.

I didn't have anywhere to go but found myself a small apartment in Melbourne. Four months later and I was cradling my first born in my arms. A little girl. A year later, she, too, was taken from me. I vowed that day that I'd never love again. But Harry and Arley made it hard to keep that vow.

Chapter One

Arley

I lit up a cigarette and rested against the leather chair in my living room. I glanced down between my legs as Harry licked up my thighs. My cock was hard and throbbing. The one thing about the bear shifter was that he sucked like a fucking hoover. He'd given me the best blow jobs I'd experienced ever in my life.

He looked up at me through his lashes as he skimmed his tongue over my balls, sucking each one into his mouth. I groaned and smiled down at him. Even though Harry was an alpha, he wasn't like other alphas I'd met. He was very submissive. Not that I was into the whole Dom/sub-life. It never really did much for me. But I was strictly a top, so it worked well that he didn't mind bottoming.

"I've been trying to talk Flynn into coming and playing with us," he murmured between licks.

I smirked. I knew that Harry had a thing for Flynn. I'd assumed they'd been playmates, but apparently, Flynn had never gone there. In fact, I was surprised when I found that the sexy little unicorn didn't play with anyone. I didn't know his story, but Harry said that Flynn didn't do one night or casual. I think Harry would have liked to make them more. I wasn't against that either.

"Have you told him how you feel?" I asked.

Harry's cheeks pinkened, and he shook his head. "No," he replied with a sigh. He sat back on his knees and looked down at his lap. "I think I might have missed my chance."

I frowned and shook my head. "What makes you say that?"

Harry shrugged his shoulders. "I don't know. I've always talked to him about playing, but I've never let him know I want more from him. He takes heat suppressants so that he can work, so he can't feel that we are fated."

"Ah," I said. "I had wondered how that happened. But I thought maybe he could be like another guy I know, Monroe, who couldn't scent the fate."

Harry nodded and sighed again. "I don't know if I fucked it up."

"Do you want me to talk to him?"

Harry smiled up at me. "Aren't you busy, though?"

I chuckled and shrugged. "Yeah, but I can find the time to talk to our mate."

"Our mate," Harry whispered. "You want both of us?"

That was the other thing that always amazed me about the bear shifter. He was so unsure of himself. He was a shrewd businessman, running a very successful party company. Put him in a suit, and you'd never realize just how vulnerable he was. But here, while we were both naked, he let it show. Beneath the tough businessman exterior, he was scared and unsure of himself. It was a bizarre contrast.

I leaned forward, stubbed my half-smoked cigarette in the ashtray beside me, and reached out my fingers to Harry's chin. I lifted his face to mine and looked into his big brown eyes. "I want both of you," I assured him.

Harry's smile lit up his face. And he bit into his bottom lip as he bounced his head up and down.

"Now, I believe my cock isn't going to suck itself," I growled.

Harry gasped and glanced down at my cock, still hard and leaking precum against my stomach.

"I want to fuck you," Harry whispered.

I growled playfully and reached over to the drawer on the table beside me. Reaching out a bottle of lube that I'd sat in when I knew that Harry was coming over, I uncapped the bottle and poured a big wad of it on my fingers.

"Stand," I directed.

Harry at once stood and turned his back to me. He bent forward, opening his self-up so that I could see his pucker. I ran my fingers down over his crack, circling his hole that trembled under my touch. Slowly I pushed one finger inside him and pressed down on his prostate, delighting in the groan that fell from Harry's lips.

I continued to work him over until I'd stretched him to three fingers. I took more lube and spread it up and down my cock.

"Come take what you need, baby," I directed.

Harry glanced over his shoulder and smiled before backing up and slowly lowering himself down. My cock pressed against the tight ring of muscles as he bored down, swallowing me deep inside him.

I groaned with the feel of his tight warm passage that massaged my cock with his every movement. Harry began to move up and down, rocking me deep inside him. I skimmed my hands up and down the stiff muscles of his back, scratching lightly over his skin. Harry moaned, and his legs began to shake.

"I'm going to cum," he moaned.

I gripped his hips firmly and fucked up deep inside him. My own orgasm was sitting right on edge. Harry roared as I felt his cum splash against my feet. I let go and sprayed him full of cum with a roar of my own.

My alpha desperately wanted to make this man our mate, but I wouldn't do it. Not until Flynn agreed to be ours.

Chapter Two

Harry

"Are you sure you don't need me to come in with you?" I asked Flynn as he wrestled with his crutches. He was about to go into the orthopedic unit to get his cast cut off.

Flynn waved his hand and shook his head. "No. You're a busy man. I'll be fine."

I rolled my eyes. "I'm never too busy for you, Flynn. How many times do I need to tell you that?"

Flynn looked up at me with those big eyes that I'd fallen in love with more and more over the five years that I'd known him. He sighed and bit into his bottom lip. I could see him wrestling with his own brain. That damned beautiful, brilliant brain of his. It stopped him from taking that final step in letting me make him mine. He overthought everything.

Flynn might have come across as a sex-crazed unicorn stripper. But in truth, he was a deep thinker. So many things scared him. He worried and worked his ass off. I didn't know what he did with his money. The house he lived in wasn't anything special, and as far as I knew, he didn't have any dependents. Not like Dylan, who used his money to pay for his dad's medical bills while he was alive.

"I'll be alright. Thank you," he said so quietly that if it wasn't for my shifter hearing, I might not have heard him.

I sighed and nodded my head. There was no point in arguing. He was as stubborn as he was beautiful. I stood watching as he hobbled his way into the hospital's main entrance before I turned and got back in the car's driver's seat.

I would put everything aside if Flynn needed me. I just needed to somehow get that through to him. I loved him. There was no question about it. I loved him more than I'd ever loved before. I just needed him to see it. I chewed on my lip as I thought about opening up and telling him exactly how I felt.

Nerves bubbled in my stomach. The thought of telling him how I felt was terrifying. I was sure that he would run if I was honest with him. I would prefer having Flynn there to work for me then never seeing him again. I sighed and briefly closed my eyes before bringing the car to life and heading toward my office.

I'd owned Reynolds catering for around seven years. I'd started it once I finished university. Having studied business, I thought the best thing I could do was start my own business. Of course, it was also the demise of my own family. My parents were disgusted at the thought that I would start a catering business that would hire, in their words, prostitutes to serve food.

They couldn't have had it more wrong, but there was not telling the great Jonathon and Judith Reynolds anything. I'd grown up with a silver spoon in my mouth; I wasn't ashamed to admit it. I was born the second son to my parents. My eldest brother Jonathon had done what was expected of him. He became a supernatural lawyer. My parents were ashamed of being supernaturals. To them, the epitome of success was to rule in a world that human's dominated. So, my father had become a neurosurgeon and at the top of his field. At the same time, my mother was a pediatrician who specialized in rare diseases that affected supernatural children.

On the surface, they appeared to be upstanding citizens who did great things for the supernatural population of Melbourne. But in truth, they were arrogant assholes who were incredibly abusive to their children and tried to turn their children into yes men. Of course, they succeeded with Jonathon. He now was a professor of law who owned his own law firm and worked with celebrities, gangsters, and the rich and corrupt of the world.

My younger sister Sofia was a cardiac surgeon and had her own clinic in Sydney. My other sister Penelope was an engineer, working overseas possibly for NASA, but I didn't really know in truth. And the youngest, Andrew. He was still in high school, but I'd heard the last time I'd spoken to Sofia for thirty seconds was that he was failing most of his classes and didn't know what he wanted to do.

I'd thought about contacting him. I'd moved out by the time Andrew was only seven years old. And when I chose to study business at university, my parents had basically turned their back on me. They pulled any funding, and I had to work part-time just to be able to afford to stay at school. Of course, they would have happily paid if I'd just chosen to go and do something that they felt was more worthy. However, I stuck to my guns. I knew what I wanted to do.

I'd always wanted to be a chef. That was what, ultimately, I would have loved to do. But I was too much of a pussy to step away too far from my parent's wishes. I'd, of course, grown up with a personal chef. I'd sneak into the kitchen to help Piper cook our meals. She knew that she would have got fired if she'd been caught. But fortunately for Piper, the last place my mother would step foot was in the kitchen. That room was far beneath her. So, every day I would learn to cook all sorts of meals. I loved it.

The next best choice that I could think of was to start a catering business that supplied food to parties, with private chefs and beautiful waiters and dancers. I was in awe at how successful the company became, and within two years, I was a millionaire. Of course, that wasn't good enough for the prestigious Jonathon and Judith. In their mind, I was no better than a pimp, offering prostitutes to horny businessmen.

They couldn't have been further from the truth. But there was no changing their minds. So, I was cast out of the family. Even my Christmas cards I might send got returned to sender. After a few years of heartache, I finally gave up and decided to build my own family. I still spoke to Sofia occasionally. Of course, it was always done in secret because if our parents ever found out that she was talking to me, they would cast her out of the family.

I sighed as I pulled into my office and stared at the building I owned. It was a large building with an industrial-sized kitchen and offices. It had a dining space and even a dance floor. I'd worked fucking hard to build what I had. I was proud of it. But it still didn't take that ache away that my parents didn't want to be a part of my life.

Chapter Three

Arley

"Thanks for coming in, everyone," Kade said with a sigh. "I swear this is doing my fucking head in."

The poor Nephilim looked exhausted. He had been working so hard on trying to end Ettore. No matter what we did, though, we were five steps behind him. We thought we would be in front with Rison and his mate Zayd and Harper in the training center. But all it did was show us how little we knew.

"So, this is what we've learned about the Hunter Island facility," Kade continued. "It seems the so-called environmental scientists working there are just a façade. Rison and Zayd said that the alphas coming out are actually scientifically created."

I frowned as others gasped around me. "How so?" Memphis, one of the shifter unit members, asked.

"Zayd has been able to find out that the omegas that are pregnant are only vessels. They aren't bred, but it is all done through I.V.F or in vitro fertilization. They breed them basically in a science lab, only placing the eggs in the omega once they are fertilized."

"So, is that what Lilibeth and Argral were doing?" Jai asked.

Kade nodded his head. "It turns out that the omegas they were using weren't impregnated, but Lilibeth and Argal were actually taking the eggs from the omegas and then sending them to one of the labs."

"Wait, one of?" Bacchus asked.

Kade sighed and nodded again. "Yes, one of. Apparently, there are many more. We are still trying to discover where. Our teams are still trying to gather information from Lilibeth and Argral. The people she was working with, Flint and Mitah, were mostly out of the knowledge loop. Lilibeth and Argral used Flint and Mitah's sperm, from what we can tell, but that was about it. Their mate, Adda, was in charge of keeping records, which is where we got a lot of information about the omegas that they'd taken eggs from. But other than that, Flint, Mitah, and Adda weren't highly involved, just stupid."

I sighed and glanced over at Bacchus. His brother Macklin had been distraught that his mate had been used. From what we'd learned, they'd planned to extract West's eggs but had been interrupted by the fact that Macklin was his mate. Lilibeth introduced them, so she only had herself to blame. It disgusted me at just how much she'd gotten away with right under our noses.

"So, what do we do now?" Coltrane asked.

"I've been working with Scout, and we have managed to get Bandit from the Onyx rebels a job on Hunter Island. Rison is still trying to find out where the other facilities are. Arcadia was able to get some information from Argral about a facility on Mangere Island, off the coast of New Zealand. It is supposed to be completely uninhabited, but from what we were able to find from Argral, there is a facility hidden there."

"Does the governments know this is happening?" Anghus asked.

Kade twisted his lips to the side and shrugged his shoulders. "I don't know for sure. I would've liked to say they have no idea, but it seems strange that they don't know about the Hunter Island facility. All emails, calls, and faxes I've sent through to the governing bodies of Hunter Island have gone unanswered."

"Shit," I said. "That makes our job even harder; if the government has given Ettore the green light to build these super alphas, how do we shut them down."

Kade nodded his head. "Yeah, that is my concern. The other concern I have is that if this other facility on Mangere Island is true, we have no jurisdiction. It is New Zealand soil; we can't even go there to investigate without New Zealand government permission."

"Fucking hell. So, what do we do?" Zion asked.

Kade ran his hands up over his face and through his hair. "This is what has been keeping me awake at night. I've been working with my daughter Ada, Merza, and my vampire team to find a solution. But without getting government bodies involved, I don't know what the answer is. Of course, as we have previously discussed, getting government bodies involved also proves to be an issue."

I nodded my head. It felt like it didn't matter what we did; Ettore would win. I believed in the prophecy that the gods would come and give their power to the children born with special powers, but it sometimes felt hopeless. Especially if governments were against us as well.

Chapter Four

Flynn

I sat in Harry's office, wincing at the state of my leg. The hair was darker, and crusty dried skin was begging to be peeled off.

"Why don't I drive you home so you can have a hot bath and soak your leg?" Harry said as he watched me glare down at my leg for what could have been the millionth time.

I sighed and glanced up at my boss and probably the one man that I felt closest to. "Maybe."

"How long do you need to use the crutches for?"

"Dr. Roberts said another two weeks, then he wants to look at it again to make sure the ligaments and stuff have all healed properly." It always pissed me off that I hadn't been able to shift. I hated it. And yet no doctor had been able to tell me why I couldn't.

"Did you talk to him about shifting?" Harry asked. I'd been forced to confess to my issue when I broke my leg. Of course, the first question everyone asked was why I couldn't shift. So, I'd told him and Dylan. It wasn't something I liked to talk about.

I bit into my bottom lip and nodded my head. "He is organizing an appointment with another doctor. A Dr. Rankin. Apparently, he is an Obgyn specializing in supernaturals. If he can't work it out, they will want to send me to Melbourne."

Shifting hadn't ever been anything important to me before. It was the last thing I wanted to do. Well, not until I broke my damned leg and couldn't shift to fix it. Harry nodded his head, and I could see him wanting to ask if he could come with me. I knew that Harry wanted me. But after Luke, I refused to acknowledge it. I wasn't going to be hurt again.

I knew Harry and I were fated mates. I knew we were meant for each other. I also knew that Arley was ours, but I held back. I couldn't stand the thought of letting either man into my heart only to have them break it again. I couldn't go through that again. Not to mention that neither man knew about the baby. I'd not told them anything. It wasn't that I didn't want them to know, but the memories were just too painful to talk about.

"Come on, I'm done here anyway. Let me take you back home, I'll run you a bath, and then I'll clean your apartment to make it easier for you to get around," Harry said as he stood and lifted his keys from his desk.

I rolled my eyes. "My apartment isn't that messy," I groused.

Harry chuckled and raised his brow at me. "Honey, the last time I was there, I thought you were attempting to grow a pot of macaroni and cheese."

I gasped and widened my eyes. "It wasn't that bad," I whined.

Harry laughed and nodded his head. "Alright, it wasn't that bad. But I'm sure you will need a change of sheets and some washing done. I'll get it done while you're in the bath. I'll even stop at the shop and get some nice oil to put in the bath."

I sighed. I had to admit that the sound of luxuriating in a hot bath with scented oils was really appealing. I'd had to tape a bag around my leg and stick it out of the shower for the last three weeks. It was starting to get on my goat, so I was looking forward to being able to soak my whole body in a deep hot bath.

I stood awkwardly on my crutches and hopped out towards Harry's car. "Are you going to replace Dylan?" I asked.

My best friend, Dylan, was now mated to one of the Devil's Advocates, Jai. They'd moved his dad, Jason, over to the Devil's Advocates compound, but sadly he'd lost his battle with cancer a few days after the move. Dylan had been destroyed. I knew that he'd be a wreck. His Papa had been Dylan's whole life. Something that I was always secretly jealous of. But now he was a Papa to the cutest little boy named Jason, and I'd convinced him with the help of Jai not to work anymore. He had better things to do than shimmy his ass in front of horny alphas.

"Yeah, I'm going to have to advertise," Harry said. I hadn't been able to dance since breaking my leg, driving me crazy. "I'm thinking of putting on a few more. We've had quite a few extra bookings lately."

I didn't necessarily love dancing. I hated it when the alphas got a little handsy. Some were even more than a little handsy. Thankfully Harry usually sent a security team with me. Zengu was worth his weight in gold. The giant troll usually just had to turn his glare onto whatever alpha was getting too touchy, and they would step back. There had only been one or two times that he had to actually step in and say something or do something to make them stop. Thankfully though, the look worked.

"Can I help with interviews?" I asked with a smile, making Harry laugh.

"Sure. I like having your opinion. You've got a good eye."

I grinned and bounced my head up and down. One thing I loved about Harry was that he did value my opinion. I never felt like I was beneath him. At times like that, I thought about going back on my decision to never get involved again.

Chapter Five

Harry

Flynn and I were sitting in my office. I'd helped him around his apartment over the last two weeks and tried to work up to telling him how I felt about him. Arley told me I just needed to rip the band-aid off and blurt it out, but that wasn't who I was. Hell, I couldn't stand up to my own parents; I wasn't going to be able to quickly tell the man I was in love with how I felt.

"Whose first?" Flynn asked.

I glanced down at the list of resumes that had come in through the week. I'd narrowed them down to four potentials. Two women and two men. One elf, a pixie, a witch, and a wolf shifter.

"An elf named Goren," I said.

Flynn hummed. "Do you know what he looks like?"

A stab of jealousy spread through me, but I pushed it aside. I had to remind myself that Flynn wasn't looking at these people as potential relationships.

"Don't know," I said as a knock sounded on my door. "I guess we will find out."

Tess poked her head into my office. "Goren is here for his interview. I've also got Tesin in reception to interview after Goren," she said with a smile.

"Thanks, Tess, send Goren in," I replied.

Tess smiled and nodded her head. When the door re-opened, a tall elf with white hair and startling blue eyes stepped in through the door. He was a very typical elf. And, of course, that meant beautiful. According to his resume, he was only nineteen and an alpha.

"Hello, Goren," I said as I stood and stuck my hand out to shake. "I'm Harry Reynolds, and this is Flynn."

Goren smiled and shook my hand before shaking Flynn's. "It's nice to meet you both."

"Have a seat, and let's chat," I said, pointing to the chair opposite as I sat back down behind my desk. "Have you ever done waiting or dancing before?"

A slight blush spread across Goren's cheeks, and he nodded his head. Licking his lips, he fidgeted. "Um, yeah, dancing. I've been working at Hellfire for the last year."

"Ah," I replied. Hellfire was a strip club run by a very unsavory troll, Theo Callaghan. Reportedly it wasn't a good place to work. It was one of those places where your feet stuck to the floor in ungodly substances. The dancers were usually coked out of their heads. But looking at Goren, he didn't have a drug problem.

"You realize that this is a drug-free zone?" I said.

Goren smiled and seemed to breathe a sigh of relief. "Yes," he replied. "I'm not on drugs. I hate them."

I smiled. "Great. So, you were a dancer at Hellfire?"

Goren bit into his bottom lip and nodded his head. It struck me as strange that he was a dancer. Most alphas didn't get work as dancers.

"I needed the money. I, um, I came from a bad life and was living on the streets."

I held my hand up. "You don't have to tell me about your past. We are a non-judgmental company. I just ask about you dancing because I want to know where you would fit. Is the dancing something you want to continue? Or are you hoping to do more waiting?"

Goren's shoulders relaxed further. "I was hoping to maybe do waiting. I will do dancing if that is what you want me to do, but I'm not very comfortable doing it."

I shook my head. "That's understandable. I will never push you to do dancing if that's not what you're comfortable with. Have you had experience in waiting before?"

Goren shook his head. "No. I was strictly a dancer at Hellfire, and that is the only place I've ever worked."

"That's fine. It's really not hard. We cater to parties, weddings, and funerals. The waiting basically is just walking around with a tray of food. It might be delivering plates of food if there is a sit-down meal, but generally, most just want finger food. As long as you can hold a tray and walk, you can do the waiting," I explained with a smile.

Goren nodded his head. "I can do that," he replied.

"Great. And this is your best number to contact you on?" I asked.

Goren glanced at the paper I'd pointed to and nodded his head. "Yes. Unless I'm at work, I'll answer, but I can call you back if you leave a message."

I smiled and nodded my head. "Not a problem. I have a couple more interviews to conduct today, and Flynn and I will decide by tomorrow, so I'll give you a ring then."

"Thank you," Goren replied as he stood from his chair. After shaking mine and Flynn's hands, he turned and left my office.

"He needs the job," Flynn said once we were alone.

I nodded my head. "He has the job."

Flynn smiled up at me, and it took everything in me not to bend forward and kiss his beautiful lips.

Chapter Six

Flynn

After interviewing all of the candidates, we decided to hire them all. They all were beautiful people who would be great for Reynolds. River, who was a witch, was going to be a dancer. She had studied dance throughout university but couldn't do ballet professionally after an injury. She didn't want to give up dance, so she thought this was the next best thing. I wasn't sure I totally agreed. But she seemed happy enough. I guessed working for Reynolds was so much better than dancing at a place like Hellfire. At least here, she would be cared for and wouldn't be groped or potentially raped.

"So, you are okay with helping River out?" Harry asked as he drove me home.

"Sure. I don't know that she'll need much help," I said.

Harry smiled. "Probably not, but I guess there is a big difference between dancing ballet and dancing sexy."

I laughed and nodded my head. "She could go and do the nutcracker on the handsy alphas."

Harry barked out a laugh. "I'll get her to teach Zengu her moves." I laughed as I envisioned the giant troll in a tutu. "When do you have to see Dr. Rankin?"

I sighed at the change in subject. I didn't want to think about the appointment that I had coming up. It didn't matter to me why I couldn't shift. I didn't want to look into it further. Partly because I was scared that it might show me something that would change my life for the worse. Sometimes ignorance was bliss.

"Tomorrow," I replied.

"What time?" Harry asked.

"Nine."

Harry nodded his head. "I'll pick you up at quarter to."

"I can take myself," I said quietly.

Harry shook his head firmly. "No. I want to be there with you. Flynn, I want to support you."

"You do support me. You are a very close friend."

Harry's body stiffened, and I frowned at his reaction. His hands tightened on the steering wheel, and his jaw tensed.

"What?" I asked.

Harry sighed and didn't say anything. He slowly pulled the car over to the curb and shut off the engine before turning to look at me.

"Flynn," he started before looking out the windscreen. "I like you, Flynn. A lot. I want to be there for you. When something happens to you, I want to help you through it."

I frowned and shook my head. "You do that."

Harry looked back at me. "Not in the way that I want to."

I shook my head with confusion. "What do you mean?"

Harry sucked in a deep breath, and his eyes roamed over my face. "I don't want to just be your friend Flynn. I want to be more than that to you. I want to be closer."

I sighed. "Harry," I started, but Harry held his hand up, stopping me.

"Can't you feel it, Flynn? We are meant to be together. We are fated."

I sighed again. "I know, Harry. But it's not that simple for me. There are things you don't know about me. I just struggle. I can't, Harry. I can't give myself over that easy."

Harry reached out for my hands and held them tightly in his. "Flynn. I'm not asking for just a quick play partner. I don't want to fuck you and then cast you away. I want you to be mine. Forever. I want to be yours. Forever."

I smiled. "I know what you mean, Harry. I like you a lot, and if there was anyone in this world that could make me change my opinion on giving myself to someone, it would be you. But it's not that simple. What about Arley?"

Harry sighed. "He is meant to be ours too."

I nodded my head. "He is meant for you. I'm not sure he is meant for me."

Harry shook his head firmly. "That's not true. He wants us both."

"For mates or for a quick play session?"

Harry winced, and I nodded my head.

"I can't do that, Harry. And I can't be with someone that isn't going to be faithful to me."

"Will you tell me your story one day?" Harry said quietly.

I nodded my head. "One day. Let's get home, so I can get some rest before the appointment tomorrow."

Harry nodded, turned in his seat, and brought the car to life before driving me home in silence. I didn't know what to say. Harry looked like he wanted to say more but wasn't willing to. The silence was uncomfortable, and it felt like our conversation was unfinished. But there was no way I would make myself vulnerable to someone who wasn't going to be just mine.

When Harry pulled into my driveway, he continued to stare out the windscreen. "I'll see you tomorrow at quarter to nine," I said, trying to appease him.

Harry turned and smiled, but the smile didn't reach his eyes. He nodded his head but still didn't say anything. I sighed and slowly made my way out of the car and towards the front door. Typically, Harry would follow me inside, and we would have dinner together or just hang out. This time was different. This time Harry didn't even turn his car off. He simply waited until I reached my front door and then reversed out of my driveway. I felt my heart crumple. *Had I fucked it up?*

Chapter Seven

Arley

"Have you and that pretty little unicorn hooked up yet?" Zion asked as we sat with our feet kicked up on the banister in front of us.

I laughed and shook my head. "Na. If we were to hook up, that would be it; I wouldn't be able to let him go," I admitted.

Zion grinned at me. "Still got his mate going on?"

I nodded my head. "Yep. He is working his way up to telling Flynn how he feels."

"What about you? Have you told Flynn how you feel?"

I shook my head. "Not yet. I'm waiting on Harry."

Zion rolled his eyes. "It's a good thing then that supernaturals live longer than humans because, by the time the pair of you get it all together, you will be an old man. You'll need Viagra just to mate with him."

I barked out a laugh and sucked down the last of my cigarette. "Never. This cock is always going to stay hard."

Zion snorted. Most of the inner members were mated and had kids of their own. It was only me, Zion and Oakland, left without mates. It was lonely. I didn't think I would ever feel this way. But it was like the more of the Devils that had children, the more I wanted a mate and a little one of my own.

"Have we heard more about what's happening with the facilities?" I asked.

Zion shook his head. "Nothing. From what I can tell, Ettore is taking his time with this one. He is still training the alphas."

"How's Harper going with it all?"

"Pax and Holland reckon we wouldn't even recognize her now. She has muscled-up and is so fucking strong."

"Shit. When did they see her?"

"Rison was able to sneak her out last week sometime. It had to be just a quick visit, but they got to see her. The kids were worried about her, I think."

I nodded my head. "Yeah, I can imagine."

I glanced up as Anghus started walking up the path towards where Zion and I were sitting. "Fella's," he said with a smile.

"Manage to sneak out for a few minutes, did you?" I asked with a laugh.

Anghus chuckled. "The kids are busy helping Jasper with Daffodil and Royal."

I grinned. I loved all the kids; they were terrific. And to see the powers they had was awe-inspiring. It made me think even more about my own children and what they would be like one day. I wondered whether I would have super powerful children like the ones born.

"Bacchus is on the phone to Kade, he reckons they've got some news, so I thought I'd come and get you all. No doubt Bacchus wants to fill you all in," Anghus said.

I nodded and stubbed my cigarette butt into the ashtray before standing along with Zion and following Anghus back to the main house. Israel, Oakland, Lynx, Miles, Corson, and Larissa were there by the time we got there.

"So, what'd he say?" Anghus asked as he walked through the living room to Bacchus.

"Rison got word that they are moving the alphas that Ettore has been working with. He is getting ready to bring a new batch earthside. Apparently, this group he is bringing has been in the underworld for the last few months and is now ready to come earthside to continue their training."

"Shit," I said with a sigh. "So, will Harper be going with the old group?"

Bacchus nodded his head. "Ettore has agreed to keep Rison and Zayd with the new group. Apparently, Zayd has proved himself a good trainer, so Ettore wants him to teach the new alphas. Rison is still looking after Mormo and Bune. From what Rison said, Ettore has taken his hands off the raising of Mormo, which has surprised us. I'm not sure if that means that he trusts Rison to raise him to be loyal to his father or what, I don't know."

"So, we will need to have someone follow the old alphas to know where they are," Israel said.

Bacchus nodded his head. "Scout will be following them. Kade believes Ettore is going to be keeping them in Lalbert. He has a house here in the forest. That was the first I heard about this house. But Kade thinks he will send at least some there."

"Do you think he is going to split them up?" I asked.

Bacchus looked over at me and nodded his head. "Yeah, I think so."

"That could put Harper in danger," Lynx said.

Bacchus sighed and nodded his head. "We will work hard to get her out or make sure she is safe."

"Does Pax and Holland know about this?" Anghus asked.

"I think so," Bacchus answered.

Anghus nodded his head. A bubble of worry went through me; I didn't want our plan to backfire. The last thing I wanted was something horrible to happen to Harper. If she was found out, it would be death for sure.

Chapter Eight

Flynn

"Flynn, come on in," Doctor Rankin called. I'd been sitting waiting nervously with Harry by my side, chewing the hell out of my bottom lip. I wasn't sure that Harry coming in was the right thing to do, but I'd been thinking more and more about what he said to me in the car.

It kept playing on my mind. I knew that we were fated. I'd have to have lost all sense of smell not to know. If it weren't for the heat suppressants that I regularly took so that I didn't go into heat for work, I would have had a horrible time.

I just couldn't get over the fear I felt, though. I couldn't go through the whole thing with Luke again. That had nearly crushed me last time. I would die if it happened again.

Dr. Rankin pointed at the empty chairs as he sat down at his desk and gave me a smile. "It's nice to meet you. Now, I've got a referral here from Dr. Roberts. Apparently, you broke your leg and were unable to shift to heal it, is that correct?"

I nodded my head and bit into my bottom lip again. "Yes, that's right." Harry's presence beside me felt comforting but looming. I wanted him to leave but be with me as well. I was completely confused about what emotion I was feeling.

"Have you ever been able to shift?" Dr. Rankin asked.

I shook my head. "No. I'd never really tried as a kid, and then a few years ago, I tried after something happened, and I found I couldn't."

Dr. Rankin nodded his head. "Was it an accident or injury that you were trying to heal a few years ago?" I glanced at Harry and sucked in a deep breath. Dr. Rankin frowned and looked between the two of us. "Flynn, would you rather this visit on your own?"

I looked between Harry and Dr. Rankin before shaking my head. "No. I, um, I just haven't told this story before."

Dr. Rankin gave me a patient smile and nodded his head. "Take your time. Get your thoughts together and only tell me about the medical things that might pertain to this."

I let out a shaky breath and nodded once more. "Six years ago, I lost my daughter to SIDs. A few months later, I tried to take my own life. I tried hanging myself. But my neighbor found me before I was dead. He pulled me down and tried to get me to shift, but I couldn't."

I couldn't look at Harry. I didn't know whether he looked at me with disgust or pity, nor could I face him to see.

"How old was your daughter?" Dr. Rankin asked.

"It was her first birthday," I replied with a hitch in my voice.

I could hear Harry breathe out slowly before I felt his hand wrap around my fingers and hold them.

"What happened after you tried to commit suicide?" Dr. Rankin asked.

"I was taken to Melbourne Hospital. I had a broken collar bone and some damage to my vocal cords. I was living in Melbourne at the time and had to stay there while I healed. Then I spent time in a mental health unit."

Dr. Rankin nodded his head. "Did anyone do tests to see why it was you couldn't shift?"

I shrugged my shoulders. "Not that I know of. But I was pretty out of it for a little while there."

Dr. Rankin nodded again. "Yes, I can imagine they had you on some fairly heavy drugs to try and stabilize your moods and pain. How long after your daughter's passing did you try suicide."

"Days. I think it was only three or four days."

"And were you mated to her father?"

I shook my head as a stab of pain ripped through me at the memory of discovering Luke fucking my mother.

"No. We were in a relationship, or so I thought."

Dr. Rankin nodded his head. "Were you tested for STIs once your relationship ended?"

I nodded my head. "Yes. I went and got all the checkups done. It all came back clean."

Dr. Rankin smiled. "Were you sexually active after the relationship ended?"

"No. I haven't been with anyone since then."

"Then we can strike out STIs as the cause. What I'm going to do is to organize some blood tests first. The fact that you were able to conceive and, I presume, carry a child through to full pregnancy tells me that it isn't a problem with your reproductive system. I would like to also perhaps do some scans. Sometimes there can be an issue in the brain, and I'd like to rule anything like that out."

I nodded my head but found I couldn't really listen. Harry hadn't said a word, but he also hadn't let go of my hand. Suddenly I found myself worrying about what he thought. I felt my anxiety begin to creep up at perhaps losing Harry. He was my best friend and, if I was frank with myself, the only man other than Luke I had ever truly loved.

Chapter Nine

Harry

I didn't know how to respond when Flynn said that he'd had a child who had died. My first reaction was jealousy. Another man had already had him. But I shook that off really quickly. Then I started to think about how when I first met Flynn, he'd literally only just lost his daughter and then tried suicide. No wonder he was so closed off; I could imagine he was still grieving.

Here I was putting pressure on him to become my mate, and he was still grieving the loss of his child. Most mating relationships resulted in pregnancy, so when I suggested he become my mate, which meant I was trying to impregnate him. I felt so stupid. Even though I couldn't have known, it didn't change how much of an idiot I felt.

The rest of the appointment went along as normal. Dr. Rankin sent off referrals and made appointments for Flynn to undergo tests. He took blood from Flynn, and then we were headed out. I didn't know what to say. But I knew I had to say something. I wanted Flynn to know that I loved him no matter what happened in his past. I wasn't going to turn my back on him.

"Flynn," I started as we sat in the car. Flynn didn't lift his head but stared down at his hands. "Look at me, Flynn." I didn't know why it was so important to have his eyes on me, but it was. Flynn lifted his head, and I could see the tears sheening in his eyes. "Oh, Flynn." I pulled him into my arms across the center console. A sob bubbled from his lips, and I pulled him tight against me.

This poor beautiful man. He'd gone through all of that grief alone. My heart was shattering at the thought. He'd kept it in for the last five years that we'd known each other. I held him tight as I stroked up and down his back. As his tears eased, I lifted his face.

"I love you, Flynn," I said quietly. Flynn's eyes widened, and his mouth opened and closed as he tried to find something to say. I shook my head. "I'm not telling you that because I want you to forget everything and let me make you, my mate. I'm telling you that because it's the truth. I want to walk this journey with you, even if that is only as a friend. No matter what. I want to walk by your side, any way you'll take me."

"Harry," Flynn began. "I am so confused by how I feel. I think I love you too. And part of me really wants to throw caution to the wind and make you, my mate. Part of me wants to say, let's bring Arley in too. But then that part of me is so frightened because of my past. Luke destroyed me."

I nodded my head. "Will you tell me what happened?"

Flynn breathed in deeply and nodded his head. "Not here. Let's go home, either yours or mine, and then we will talk."

I nodded my head and released Flynn so that I could bring the car to life. I took Flynn's hand as I started towards his home. I felt that maybe he might have been more comfortable in his space. My head couldn't even understand that he told me he might love me and even want Arley. I didn't know what to do with that information. But at that moment, it wasn't necessary.

I pulled into Flynn's driveway and killed the engine. Glancing over at him, I could see his anxiousness. I knew that his story was going to be a painful one. Whatever Luke did to him was terrible. And I was going to have to keep hold of my alpha to prevent him from hunting the fucker down and killing him.

Once inside the house, Flynn went to a shelf and pulled out a shoe box. He opened it and inside were photos. He lifted the pictures and handed them to me. They were all of a baby with blonde curls; her blue eyes sparkled with mischief as she smiled up at her father behind the camera.

"That is Albany, my daughter," Flynn said with a warm smile.

"She was beautiful. I can definitely see that you were her father," I replied.

Flynn nodded his head. "I was so glad that she came out looking like me." He sucked in a deep breath and fingered one of the photos as he stared at his daughter with glassy eyes. "I haven't looked at these photos in over a year. I think about her every day, but it was becoming too hard to keep looking at the pictures. I miss her so fucking much. She was the best thing to ever happen to me."

I reached out my hand and took his hand in mine. "Never feel like you can't talk to me about her. I want to hear about her."

Flynn looked up at me and smiled. "She was born into so much heartache. I don't know why the creator allowed her to live. Especially when they took her from me only a year later."

I sighed and nodded my head. "Sometimes life is so fucking cruel."

Flynn nodded his head. "My mother was an alcoholic. She would get clean now and then but inevitably get back on the booze. She'd been clean for about two months when I was eighteen. I came home and found her passed out in a pile of vomit. Luke was sitting on our couch. He'd said he found her walking naked outside. I don't know if that was totally true now that I look at it with hindsight. It turns out she'd drank a bottle of vodka and taken many pills. Anyway, Luke and I started getting closer. Our relationship was completely platonic at first. He helped me with my Mama. He lived only a few houses down. I'd go there when I needed a break. Eventually, one night we had sex and started our relationship."

I bit down on my lip to stop the jealousy from showing. I didn't know anything about Flynn's family. It wasn't something that he'd ever talked about. I had figured he hadn't been raised in a happy family. But didn't know anymore.

"Anyway, we were together about a year when I found out I was pregnant with Albany. I was so excited. It was the next step in our relationship. I wasn't mated to him. But I wanted to be. He kept promising one day. But it never happened. I can see why now, but at the time, I believed that he needed time. Anyway, I went over to see him, but he wasn't home, so I went back to my house. I heard my mother fucking someone, which wasn't unusual; she often brought men home when she was drunk. However, when I walked in, I realized it was Luke, she was fucking. It destroyed me. I walked past them, gathered up my clothes, and left the house. My mother never saw me. But Luke watched me with a smile the whole way. Then just as I was about to walk out the fucking door, he gave my mother the mating bite."

Flynn's voice hitched, and a growl fell from my lips. That cunt. I pulled Flynn into my arms and held him.

"I'm so fucking sorry, Flynn. No wonder you didn't want to get involved in a relationship again," I said quietly as I held him and kissed the top of his head.

If I ever had the misfortune of meeting Luke or Flynn's mother, I might be inclined to shred them to pieces. I couldn't understand how anyone could be so fucking cruel.

Chapter Eleven

Arley

"Right, listen up, everyone," Kade said as he bustled into the shifter unit at the AJE authority precinct. "I've got the news that Ettore plans to move out the alphas today. Here is what we know. They are being moved to several houses all over Victoria. There are seven houses in Lalbert, two in Winchester, and five in Augusta."

"How many alphas to each house?" Memphis asked.

"Five alphas to a house. Harper is being moved to one here in Lalbert. It is the house that Ettore has used while he was in Morpheus."

"Where is Ettore staying?" I asked.

"At the training center. Rison and Zayd are staying at the training center too. They will be charged with training the new alphas meant to arrive tomorrow from the underworld. There will be a total of sixteen new alphas arriving tomorrow."

"That's a small group," Zion said.

Kade nodded his head. "Rison doesn't know a lot about this new lot. What Zayd knows is that this lot is all warlocks. They are coming from a facility off the coast of South Africa. Seal Island. I've had a brief look at the maps, and from what I could see, it isn't a habited island. Tourists visit to see the seals, but I'm not sure about a facility."

I hummed. "Are these alphas produced from Nystrom?" I asked.

"I'm assuming so, but I can't be sure. I'm not even sure how we can find out not unless we research the island ourselves. But once again, we don't have authority because the Island is part of South Africa."

I ran my hands up over my face; it seemed that there was no easy way to find answers. Ettore had covered his ass too well. We needed to somehow get our own alphas that had powers to read minds. Harper was strong. But her powers were in her strength.

"We need to infiltrate more," I said.

Kade nodded his head. "That's what I've been thinking. Unfortunately, the kids are still too young to get in there. There is one demon who I think would be ideal, but she is only fifteen and obviously female. Both of which are not useful for us. However, she can see past wards and read minds. She is the only one I've heard of that has been able to read Ettore's mind."

I winced, and as I looked around, I could see the look on the other's faces. "I hate to say this, but could she seduce Ettore? For one night? Get all the information she could get."

Kade sighed. "If she was over eighteen, I would be more inclined to suggest it, but I don't want to do that because she is so young." Kade scrubbed his hands over his face.

"What has Bandit found?" Memphis asked.

"So far, not a lot. He is still in the training stages of the facility, but he was able to confirm what Israel saw with the omegas. But that's it so far."

"We are behind him again," Coltrane growled.

"Yeah, it seems that way. I don't want to give up yet. But we are definitely going to have to keep researching."

"Can we perhaps get some others into the other facilities? Maybe Rison can find out from Ettore where the other facilities are? Can we do like we have with Bandit? Onyx Rebels have a lot of human members. Can we place someone in each facility to gather information?" I asked.

Kade nodded his head. "I think that is going to be our next bet. I'm working on gathering a group of human cops to go undercover. But I'm thinking of also sending a few more alphas. I've been meeting with Scout and Hawke, and they are prepared to send in some alphas that work for the rebels."

"We've got some that we could send in, too," Anghus said.

Kade nodded his head. "I think we can work it. Let's gather up an undercover team that we can train to send in. This isn't going to move quickly, which I know is fucking frustrating. But we have to remember that this war will not be won until the children are older."

I nodded my head. I hated it. I wanted to go and end Ettore at once. But I also knew that even if we were to kill Ettore, there would be another to take his place. We had to be patient and wait for the prophecy to play.

"In other news, Alan Carmichael is being released from prison next month. We are going to have a tail on him. I don't trust that Ettore won't try to connect with him again."

A growl sounded around the room at the name of one of the Morpheus member's release.

Chapter Ten

Flynn

Harry stayed with me for the rest of the day after my confession. I was so conflicted about how I felt. He talked to me about Arley. I knew that the three of us were fated; I was able to scent that. But my fears of being hurt again were what held me back from taking that next step. When I admitted as much, Harry said he understood. He opened up to me and told me about his family and how they had turned their back on him.

He told me about his brother Andrew and the troubles that he was having. I encouraged Harry to reach out to Andrew. I felt for him. I hated that parents could love so conditionally. I hadn't spoken to my mother since I left. As far as I could tell she never even tried to reach out to me.

I did think about contacting her when Albany was born and then again when Albany died, but I stopped myself. *What would she say?* I wondered if she was still mated to Luke. I pondered if she was still drinking or even alive. Sometimes I was curious and thought about tracking her down. But that logical part of my brain always stopped me. They hurt me. In the most horrific way; they didn't deserve to know how good I was doing.

"Hey, how are you feeling?" Harry asked when I walked out of my room bleary-eyed the following day.

I smiled and breathed a breath of relief to know that Harry stayed. He didn't try to sleep in the bed with me and stayed on the couch. It must have been horribly uncomfortable for him. Still, it made me trust him even more, knowing that he wasn't using my confession as a way to weasel his way in.

I should have known that Harry wasn't that man to manipulate. He hadn't tried anything for five years. I knew that he was my mate the day I met him. I also knew he realized it too, yet he was prepared to stand back and allow me to make the first move. Even after five years when I hadn't, he still waited patiently.

I think that was what made me fall in love with him. But that little bit of fear that I had still held me back. It wasn't necessarily that I was worried that he would cheat on me. It was the fact that I knew if I mated with Harry, I would fall pregnant. I couldn't go through it again if I lost another child. My heart wouldn't be able to take it. I know that SIDs were one of those things that you couldn't predict. I did everything the doctors and nurses told me to do. I made sure Albany didn't have blankets; she didn't sleep on her belly. I did everything right, or so I thought. But she still died.

It was something I knew I'd never survive if it happened again. I sighed and smiled wearily at Harry. "I'm alright. I feel like I've been run through the wringer."

Harry smiled and nodded his head. "You shed a lot of emotions yesterday. You've been carrying that around on your own for a long time. I'm not surprised you were exhausted."

"Yeah, I slept like a log last night."

"I bet. I, um, well, I've been giving a bit of thought to Andrew. I think that I might try and contact him. If what Sofia said is true and he is starting to go down a destructive path, I think I can prevent that."

I smiled at Harry and nodded my head. "I'm glad. I'll support you. Even if you just need to vent. I'm here."

"Thank you," he said before slapping his knees and standing from the couch. "How about I make us some breakfast, and then we go into the office. You have to start training River today, and I've got to get the shopping list set for the Lalbert footy club dinner on Saturday."

I groaned. "I hate working with them."

Harry chuckled and nodded his head. "I know you do. I'm thinking I'm going to send Reuban. He likes working with them, and they love that little twink."

I laughed and nodded my head. "He only likes them because he likes Tom, the captain."

Harry grinned. "Yeah, I think Tom stops everyone from touching him. But I'm not keen on sending River in yet. I want to train her a bit before we send her in. This will be a good chance for Goren and Tesin to start on the waiting, along with Alexi and Dondra."

I nodded my head. Alexi and Dondra were twin brothers, wolf shifters. They had been working for Reynolds longer than even I had. They only ever did waiting, but they were popular. They were typical meat heads and full of muscles, but everyone seemed to love them. They were great workers, too, making it easy for Harry to send them.

Chapter Eleven

Arley

"I'm going to go over to Harry's. Are you going to need me for a few hours?" I said to Anghus as I walked towards my bike at the AJE authority precinct. I hadn't heard from Harry or Flynn in at least a week. We'd been working nonstop with these new alphas coming up and making sure that Harper was safe. We were trying to get her out. That in itself was turning into a cluster fuck.

Anghus smirked at me. He shook his head. "Go on, take off, man, fuck your man."

I barked out a laugh. I hadn't fucked anyone for weeks, not since I'd seen Harry last. But between my schedule and his, we hadn't had time to see each other. I hadn't even heard from him in at least a week. I realized how long it had been last night and gave him a ring. Apparently, stuff had happened with Flynn, and they dealt with some things.

I felt jealousy surge through me; they were purposely leaving me out. But after I talked it out with Zion, I was able to see that I just hadn't been available to them. I wanted to change that. It was time to finally lay it all out on the table and tell them how I felt. I was sick of playing this game. I didn't want them just to fuck. I wanted them as my men. Forever.

I roared through the streets of Lalbert. My bike vibrated beneath me, and the growl from the exhaust rattled through the building's windows. It always made me feel so free when I was riding. It was why I joined the Devil's Advocates in the first place. I needed that feeling of being alive. I'd been dead too long.

As soon as I met Anghus, my world changed. I became free. I learned what it was like to have a family that loved me unconditionally. Such a rare feeling compared to where I'd come from. I shook my head to shake away the memories of my fucked up childhood.

Pulling into Harry's driveway, I saw that Harry's car was parked in front of his garage. I hoped that Flynn was there too. It wasn't just Harry I needed to talk to. I needed them both. I killed the bike's engine and climbed off, walking up to the front door; I reached for the bell and gave it a ring, waiting for Harry to open it.

I was surprised when I saw Flynn's beautiful face in the open doorway. "Arley," he said with a smile before stepping into my body and wrapping his arms around my waist.

"Well, hello to you too, little one," I murmured into his hair. I was still slightly amazed. It was the first time I'd ever received any touch from Flynn. He usually got flustered around me or was stand-offish. He never instantly reached out for affection. "How about we go inside. There is a lot I need to talk to you and Harry about."

Flynn stepped back and nodded his head. "I have some things I need to say too."

I smiled and followed Flynn inside. Harry was standing in the doorway between the front door and the living room. He looked at me with a knowing smirk on his lips, and I wondered exactly what had happened since I'd been working.

"Hey, baby," I said, leaning forward and pressing a kiss on Harry's lips.

"Hi," he breathed as he returned my kiss.

"What's going on here?" I asked.

Harry chuckled. "Flynn and I have been doing a lot of talking. I think we should listen to what Flynn has to say first," he said with a wink.

I nodded and glanced over to the unicorn pacing across the living room floor and chewing on his thumb nail. I moved into the living room and sat down on the couch.

"Flynn, sweetheart," I said, gently drawing his attention to me. "You can tell me whatever you want to say. I will never judge you. It won't change how I feel about you."

"I don't know how you feel about me," he said quietly.

"Then I'm an idiot for not showing you."

Flynn stopped his pacing and looked at me with a slight frown.

"I should have told you both a long time ago. But I decided to wait and give you both time to decide. I want both of you. A lot. Not just for sex. I want to mate with you both," I said with a rush of words. I didn't realize how nervous I was to say it until it came out of my lips.

Flynn's smile was dazzling as he looked at me. Suddenly, a chuckle fell from his lips, turning into a belly laugh and a total knee-slapper laugh. I frowned and looked between him and Harry.

"He has been worried that you only wanted him for sex. " Harry chuckled. "This is just all his nervous energy finally bubbling out."

Flynn sighed and breathed out slowly. Tears leaked from the corner of his eyes. "You might not want me when you find out I'm used."

My frown deepened, and I shook my head. "What do you mean?"

Flynn sighed again, and the smile that had been so dazzling turned into a frown; the tears of laughter were soon replaced by tears of sadness. Whoever put those fucking tears there would fucking die. Anger started to bubble in my chest.

Flynn turned suddenly and went to the coffee table, where there was an open shoe box I hadn't noticed before. He reached in and pulled out a photo before handing it to me. I glanced at the picture of the most beautiful little girl with blonde curls and big blue eyes. There was no denying who her father was.

"That's Albany. My daughter. She's dead."

My frown deepened, and I glanced up at Flynn. "What happened?"

"She died of SIDs," Flynn replied.

"Oh, baby. You thought that would change how I feel about you?" I said as I stood and reached out for Flynn, pulling him into my arms. "Never. Never would that have ever changed how I feel about you."

"Even the fact that another man had given me a child?"

"Even then. Although I want to kill the fucker for touching you. But I will never judge you for being with others before I knew you, baby. Never."

Flynn breathed out and continued to let me hold him tight to my chest. My heart broke for him. I wondered if Harry knew about the baby. He hadn't told me which made me think he hadn't known.

Chapter Twelve

Flynn

Harry and I had spent about a week just talking to one another. Obviously, we had to work in between that time. But every night, I would go back to his house, or he would come to mine. He never pushed me to do anything, and we always slept in separate beds. He encouraged me to talk more about Albany. With every word I shared, it got easier. It wasn't as painful to talk about her.

Of course, it was still hard to think about Luke and Mama without feeling that stab of pain, but I guessed that was something that was always going to be there. I hoped that the sting of betrayal would disappear one day, but it wasn't yet. However, the more I shared with Harry, the more I realized that Luke and Mama had been together for the entire time. All those times that I'd see him coming out of Mama's room when I came home and believing him when he said he was just checking on her.

I'd always find the baggies of coke on the coffee table that weren't there before he came over. He was just using me. That thought made me sick with anger. But like Harry said, I got Albany from him. That was at least the bright side until it wasn't. I loved that little girl wholeheartedly, and I was prepared to be everything she needed.

I would never understand why the gods stripped her from me. But at least with Harry, I was starting to be able to focus on the good. The time I did have her. I'd spent so much time not thinking about it that I only focused on the grief. I'd put all her photos away in the shoe box, and I never looked at them. It was too painful. But slowly, I started to think I didn't have to do that anymore. I could celebrate that I had this child, and I loved her.

When Arley came, I didn't know what came over me, but I just needed to feel his arms around me. I needed to know that he wouldn't hate me. I thought maybe it was because of the mating bond. But I wasn't totally sure. Harry and I had done a lot of talking about that too. I knew I was fated for both of them. And I knew that they were both destined for each other.

"We have been talking a lot over the last week about this relationship," Harry said as we sat on the couches in his living room.

Arley had just finished looking at every photo I had stored in the shoe box and encouraging me to display them in frames. He said that Albany was too pretty to be stored in a box. I agreed with him. And promised that I would get some shelves to put them up.

"Oh yeah? And what have you discovered?" Arley asked.

Harry looked over at me, and I nodded my head. "I know that I'm fated to both of you. And I know that you are fated to each other."

Arley smiled and nodded his head. "That is true. However, after hearing your story," Arley began. I winced, expecting him to tell me that he didn't want us anymore. The look on Harry's face said the same thing. "I am worried that you will struggle if you know that Harry and I are having sex without you present."

I breathed a long breath when I realized he wasn't ending things. I nodded my head. "I don't know how I will feel. I've done things that I didn't think I would be able to do."

"Like what?" Harry asked.

I chuckled as I thought about the times I'd played with Dylan and Jai. We didn't touch. Dylan loved being watched. So, I'd jerk off while he did or while they fucked.

"You have me very curious now," Arley said with a raised brow, making me laugh.

I shook my head. "I haven't had anyone touch me since Luke. But Dylan and I jerked off together a few times, and one time he and Jai fucked while I watched."

Arley's eyes widened, and Harry gasped. "So, you like watching?" Arley asked.

I shrugged my shoulders. "I guess so. I don't know. I didn't feel anything for Dylan or Jai, so maybe that was why."

"What if," Harry started before biting into his lip. "What if Arley and I just sort of did some things. Like we don't have to fuck, but just do some things to see how you go?"

I twisted my lips to the side and nodded my head. The truth was it was turning me on. The fact that both of these men wanted me and each other was a turn-on to me. I'd jerked off many nights with the thought of the three of us together. It wasn't something I'd ever shared with Harry. I'd got through the last five years being flirty and pretending that I fucked anything with two legs. But the truth was that I kept all my fantasies hidden.

I nodded my head. "I think I'd like that."

"And if you want to join in, you can. Or if you would like to jerk off, I know I'd really like to see that," Arley said with a wicked grin.

I laughed and nodded my head. My cock was already throbbing in my pants. I knew that there wasn't going to be a chance I wouldn't jerk off.

Chapter Thirteen

Harry

I looked over at Arley, who smiled a grin, dripping with sex and promise. My cock pulsed in my jeans. It had been so fucking long since I'd played with Arley, and I knew just how wickedly fucking good he was. The vampire leaned over and licked up the side of my neck to my ear. He slipped his tongue around my lobe before nipping it hard enough to draw a blood drip with his fang.

My eyes rolled in my head, and I groaned. When I opened my eyes again and looked over at Flynn, he watched us with his lips open and his eyes hooded. I never expected him to get off on watching us. I was sure that he would feel jealousy. I worried that it would remind him too much of his ex.

"Relax," Arley whispered. "He'll tell us if it is too much."

I groaned as Arley ran his fingers across the front of my throat and squeezed tight enough to cut off my air slightly. He chuckled as he sucked on the sensitive skin of my neck and skimmed his fang over the pulse that was hammering. I continued to watch Flynn, reaching down to unbutton his jeans.

Flynn wrestled with his jeans and boxers, slipping them down to his thighs. His cock, long and hard, bounced against his abdomen. I groaned, longing to lick up the length of his cock. The scent of his slick filled the air making my cock even harder.

Arley turned his attention to Flynn and smiled. "Fuck, he is beautiful," he groaned.

Flynn's cheeks tinted. "I can't wait for the day I'm allowed to taste him," I admitted.

"I'd love to watch that. Fuck, just thinking of you on your knees in front of him, begging him to give you his cock. He'd stand over you and run his hand up and down his shaft, dripping his pre-cum over your lips until you begged just right," Arley described.

I groaned at the images that it was bringing forward. It was no hidden fact that I was submissive. Although we never went into the whole BDSM lifestyle, I wasn't interested in that. But I did like being ordered around in the bedroom.

"Would you like that, Flynn?" Arley asked.

Flynn bit into his bottom lip and nodded his head.

"I'd like to see you fuck Harry. He likes having his ass fucked hard. Have you ever been a top Flynn?" Arley asked.

Flynn and I moaned simultaneously. "No," Flynn whispered.

"Would you like to feel the power of being on top?"

Flynn nodded his head again. Arley chuckled and turned to me. "Would you like him to fuck you, Harry? Would you like to feel his cock stretching your hole? Making way for my cock? Or maybe we could both fuck you. Stretch you nice and wide. Have you gaping."

"Fuck," I moaned, and my eyes rolled in my head. I grasped my shaft through my jeans. I might explode in my pants like a teenager if I didn't get some relief soon.

Arley chuckled again. "See all the fun we could have, Flynn?"

Flynn moaned, and when I opened my eyes again, he was stroking his shaft. The scent of his slick was heady. He'd wrestled his jeans off and had his legs thrown over the edge of the chair, opening himself.

Arley stroked his hand down my front and unzipped my jeans, releasing my cock with a bounce. He pulled my jeans from my legs and rubbed his hand over my shaft to cupping my balls. I couldn't take my eyes off Flynn as he moved his fingers from his shaft down over his taint to his hole, leaking a stream of slick.

I groaned as Flynn stroked his fingers through the slick and brought them to his mouth, sucking his fingers clean.

"Fuck, that was hot," Arley moaned. I nodded my head in response and looked over at Arley, who stood and stripped from his clothes.

The vampire was sexy as hell. His cock was thick, uncut, and veiny. It hit every spot that brought me off quickly. Dark hair lightly smattered over his chest, leading down to that happy trail and v that disappeared into his jeans.

"Tell Harry what you want him to do, Flynn," Arley directed.

"I want him to suck your balls," Flynn automatically replied.

I didn't even have to think about it. I instantly fell to my knees in front of Arley and opened my mouth. Licking around his balls and down to his taint before licking back up to the base of his shaft. I sucked each ball into my mouth and hummed, feeling them jump against my tongue.

"Such a good boy," Arley said as he threaded his fingers through my hair and held me tight against his body.

I swirled my tongue all over his balls. My saliva dripped from my lips and chin.

"What else, Flynn? What else do you want him to do?" Arley asked.

"I want him to eat your ass," Flynn responded.

Arley smiled down at me, and I nodded my head. I loved that. Even though Arley was acting in charge, I still had a choice. The vampire turned and walked towards Flynn. "I'm not going to touch you, but I'm going to lean over you. Is that okay?"

"Yes," Flynn answered at once.

Arley placed his hands beside where Flynn's legs were hanging on the arms of the chair. He leaned forward so that his face was close to Flynn's. He widened his legs so that he was open to me. I kneeled forward and pressed my face between his cheeks, lapping over his hole and down over his taint.

Arley moaned. "Fuck, that feels good; stick your tongue inside me."

I groaned as I did as directed. Soon, Arley was rocking back against my face and moaning.

"I'm gonna cum," Flynn said desperately.

"I want to feel your cum on my cock," Arley said.

Flynn let out a long moan, and the scent of his cum hit my nostrils. It was enough for me to lose all control. I tongued Arley's ass like a starving man.

"Fuck yes, right there," Arley roared as he reached around and palmed his cock. "Fuck I'm going to cum."

Arley's alpha rippled through the room as cum sprayed from my cock in response. I sat back and closed my eyes. Fuck I needed more of that.

Chapter Fourteen

Flynn

I expected to feel guilty or weird after our experience, but none of that came. Instead, I felt like it hadn't been enough. My heart wanted more. Even my brain wasn't shouting as loudly now about holding back. The more time passed, the more I wanted to make Harry and Arley mine.

I had expected to feel jealous when I saw Harry and Arley together. Instead, I was so turned on. Even as I thought about them fucking while I wasn't around, it didn't bother me but spurred me on. I loved that Arley seemed to take on a natural leadership role. And I loved that Harry was so fucking submissive.

It was something I'd never experienced before. Luke had decided I was a bottom, and there was no getting around that. He would be commanding and sometimes even downright abusive during our sex. It was so different with Harry and Arley. Arley cared about both of our pleasures.

I sat watching River go through the steps that she'd been practicing. She had her first job coming up on the weekend. She was nervous, but my brain was still firmly focused on Arley and Harry. In fact, it was all I'd been able to think about day and night for the last week since our experience.

There had been not an ounce of awkwardness. We'd made dinner together, eaten, laughed, and chatted. Arley filled us in on what he was doing with the AJE authority. He told us all about Ettore and how much they wanted to bring him down. He hinted how much Dylan would love it if I agreed to move out to the compound.

Part of me had wanted to at once say yes. But my brain kept saying to just wait. I knew it was fear that stopped me. However, Arley and Harry were prepared to wait for me. Hell, Harry had waited for me for five years. I knew that he was patient. I think that is what made me love him even more.

I hadn't admitted my love to Harry, but I knew that I was close to it.

"Are you even listening?" River said.

I blinked and looked at the witch who stood with her hands on her hips and tapping her foot. I shook my head. "Sorry, what were you saying?"

River rolled her eyes and huffed. "I wondered whether I perhaps throw in a few more professional ballet moves?"

I hummed. "Show me."

River smiled and instantly moved through the start of her routine before switching into a few moves that I didn't know the names for but knew were ballet steps. They worked well with the performance. They showed off her legs and core strength, and I knew that any person watching would be turned on by her dance.

I nodded my head. "Definitely. They work perfectly with your routine."

River grinned and came and sat down beside me, bumping her shoulder with mine. "So, what has got your head off with the fairies?"

I chuckled and shook my head. "Has it been that obvious?"

"Just a little for the last week."

I barked out a laugh. "Well, for one, I've had many tests to find out why I couldn't shift. I get the results soon, and I'm nervous about that."

"Is Harry going to go with you?"

I smiled and nodded my head. "Yeah, I think so."

"I'm guessing the rest has to do with the fact that the two of you are fated mates but haven't mated yet?"

My eyes widened, and I gasped. "How did you know?"

River barked out a laugh. "Psychic? Well, no, not really. More like you two are obviously in love with each other, but neither wears a mating mark."

I sighed and nodded my head. "Yeah, that would be because of me. I was scared for so long. But I'm becoming less scared."

"What were you scared of?"

"That he would betray me."

River winced. "Sounds like you've been hurt like that before."

I nodded my head.

"Well, if it is of any comfort, my power as a witch is clairvoyance, and I can tell you that you, Arley, and Harry will live a very long and happy life together."

My eyes widened. I didn't know how River knew Arley. He'd never been in, and I'd never mentioned him.

River giggled and stood from where she sat and went back to the center of the room to go through her routine once more. My mind floated over her words. *I knew that witches were often psychic, but could she be right? Could my life really be that good?*

Chapter Fifteen

Arley

There was no wiping the smile off my face. Even Zion noticed as I walked into the dining hall the morning after.

"Someone got lucky, huh?" he said with a laugh.

I chuckled. "Yep. But in more ways than that."

Zion's eyes widened. "Wait, you're mated?"

I shook my head. "No. I'm hoping it won't be much longer. But Flynn opened up a lot about what he'd been through. Harry and he had spent the last week talking a lot."

"Yeah. He had a rough life?"

I nodded my head and sighed. "Yeah, sadly. It's not my story to tell. But I understand why he has held himself back."

Zion nodded. "I get it, man."

That was the beauty of the Devil's Advocates. We'd all had shitty lives. If we weren't raised by Morpheus, we were raised in the foster care system or, like me, with just cunts for parents that I ran away from when I was fourteen. I was lucky I found Declan and Lynx on my first night on the streets. I don't know what might've happened had they not stumbled on me rifling through a dumpster looking for something to eat.

That wasn't even the first time I'd had to look for something in a rubbish bin to eat. Growing up with junkies for parents meant there was rarely any food in the house. If I didn't steal it, I had to find it somehow. I didn't like stealing food; I always hated the thought that I was taking from someone's livelihood. But sometimes, I wasn't left with a choice. Especially after the bins had been picked up. I always tried to only steal little things, like a piece of fruit or something. Just enough to get through until I could get to school and tell my teacher I'd forgotten my lunch.

I think she always knew where I'd come from. She always had an extra sandwich packed for me. When I went up in grades, I couldn't go to her anymore. Somehow though, all my teachers still looked out for me. They would slip me a sandwich or a piece of fruit.

I was born a vampire, which meant I didn't rely on blood to thrive. In fact, I hated the taste of blood. So, I always tried to avoid it. Even as a kid, I preferred to eat food than drink blood. Sometimes I thought it would have been easier for me if I had been made a vampire and desired blood to live; that way, I wouldn't have experienced hunger for most of my childhood.

But as born vampires, we are basically the same as anyone else. The only difference is that we get more energy if we take blood or energy from someone. It was why I love sex. The energy I get from sex is so much better than that of blood. Of course, we have other powers. I'm a lot faster than others and stronger. The sun does hurt; I wear glasses and hoodies when I'm out in the sun. But I can eat garlic and crosses, of course, don't scare me. As for a stake in the heart, that would kill anyone.

My parents were both born vampires. Lucinda and Rodney. Pair of bastards. I refused to call her Mama; Lucinda wasn't as bad as Rodney. But by the time I was seven years old, I'd been passed around to most of his friends and fucked by him just about every night. Pedophilic cunts that deserve a scorching place in hell. When I finally left, it was to a blazing inferno in the house.

I should've felt guilty. I mean, I literally murdered two people. But I didn't care. They were much better off dead. I sighed and shook my head, shaking off the thoughts of the past. They were people that didn't deserve my concerns anymore.

"Any news on Harper?" I asked as I bit into the apple I'd grabbed.

Zion nodded his head. "Scout and Hawke are planning on pulling her out tomorrow."

"Can they do it safely?"

Zion nodded but then shrugged his shoulders. "I'm hoping so, but I don't know for sure. Apparently, though, they haven't been left with many choices. The house that they are in is tiny. They have to share bedrooms and a bathroom. It's too hard to hide her true identity."

I winced. The idea that anyone might find out that Harper wasn't Ryker was a scary thought. What they would do to her would be horrible.

"What are they planning?"

Zion shrugged his shoulders. "Don't know for sure. Anghus might know." Zion waved Anghus over, and when the gargoyle sat down opposite, he asked what the president knew.

"They are going in as the AJE authority. They are going to arrest the household," Anghus said.

My eyes widened, and I gasped. "Is that wise? To let Ettore know that we are on to him?"

Anghus sighed and shrugged. "I don't know. But Kade reckons this is the only way to do it safely. The only other choice is to kill the other alphas, but that's obviously not the right thing to do either."

I nodded my head. The alphas that Ettore was breeding were innocents. Caught up in a war that they didn't ask for. It wasn't fair to go and slaughter them. That would make us as bad as Ettore.

"At least this way, it gives us a chance to question the alphas and find out where they are coming from and what they know," Zion said.

"Yeah, that's true. I just hope they can get Harper out of there without any issue." I nodded.

"Me too. That's what is worrying me. I'm also a bit worried about when they bring her and whether she will be able to cope. From what Arcadia said, Ryker was a part of her now, and I don't know if that is a good thing."

I winced at the thought. "Fuck man, this is a cluster fuck."

Anghus nodded and sighed.

"Does Iver have any insight?" Zion asked.

Anghus shook his head. "I haven't really asked him. I'm trying not to use him in this sort of thing. I don't want him to feel responsible."

"That's understandable. Let him be a kid for as long as possible," I replied.

"Yeah. He is already so grown up. It scares me."

Chapter Sixteen

Harry

I felt like my head was in a daze as I went through the routine at work. I couldn't get over how beautiful Flynn looked as he pleasured himself. I've never jerked off to one thought so much in all my life. I couldn't wait for the day that I could finally call him mine. I wasn't going to push him. I knew that he would make the decision eventually, but I wanted it to be his decision.

I was sitting in my office rubbing my temples. The worst part of owning my own business was the paperwork. I fucking hated it. I could probably afford a bookkeeper to do it all for me, but I was also a control freak. A knock on the door sounded, and when the door opened, I was surprised to see Tess stick her head through the gap.

"Hey Harry, you have a visitor," she said with a smile that I couldn't quite read.

"Who is it?" I asked. If it were Flynn or Arley, they usually just let themselves in, so I knew it wasn't either of them. And I wasn't expecting anyone.

"He said his name is Andrew," Tess said. "Poor kid looks scared out of his mind."

My eyes widened, and I gasped. "Send him in."

Tess smiled and nodded her head. When the door opened again, Andrew walked through with black eyes and a nose that looked like it was definitely broken.

"Shit, Andrew, what happened?" I asked as I stood from my desk and raced to my brother's side.

He winced as I placed my arm around his ribs. Easing off my hold, I guided him over to one of the more comfortable chairs in my office.

"Dad happened," he said quietly as tears welled up in his eyes and dribbled down over his cheeks.

"He did this to you?" I asked as I gently lifted his chin to look at his face.

"No. One of the goons that work security at the house, but they said Dad ordered it. Plus Dad was there watching, he never stopped it."

A growl fell from my lips as anger built up inside my chest. It was one thing for our parents to cut us out of their lives if they didn't want us, but Dad and Mama had never laid a finger on any of us. Technically, I suppose they hadn't laid a finger on Andrew either. Not if one of the security men did. I had always hated them, but Dad insisted that he needed them. I'm not sure when a brain surgeon required security, but apparently, my father did.

"What happened? Tell me everything," I said as I sat down in the seat opposite him.

Before Andrew could start talking, my office door opened, and Tess came in holding an ice pack in her hand. She wrapped it in a tea towel and gently handed it to Andrew. "Put this on your face, sweetheart; it will keep the swelling down."

Andrew took the ice pack with thanks and gently laid it against his eye. "Thank you, Tess," I said as my receptionist squeezed my shoulder before leaving the office.

"Alright, tell me everything that happened," I started again.

Andrew sighed. "I told Dad last night that I wasn't going to go to university. I was going to culinary school. He flipped his shit and told me that if I did that, I might as well move out and not come back because I would no longer be any son of his. I told him that I would happily move out. I went upstairs to go and pack my things. When I came back to go out the front door, Reece grabbed me from behind and just started pummeling me. Finally, when I was about to lose consciousness and couldn't stand, Dad told him to stop. Reece and Dad walked away and just left me there on the floor. Mama watched the whole thing and didn't do anything to stop them. When I could stand up again, I rang Sofia and asked her for your address. I got on the bus and came here."

I wanted to drive straight to Melbourne and put a bullet between my father's eyes. I couldn't describe the white-hot fury prickling all over my skin. What kind of bastard does this to his own son.

"Do you want to lay charges?" I asked.

Andrew sighed again and shook his head. "What would the point be? He would get away with it. He'd just blame Reece, and nothing would happen to him."

I sighed. "I know. It might put a spotlight on him, though."

Andrew shrugged his shoulders. "It doesn't matter. I'll alter once my head stops spinning for three seconds, and it will be alright."

I nodded my head, wondering why he hadn't altered at once. It made me wonder if he'd tried and couldn't.

"Is it alright that I stay with you?" he asked. The vulnerability in his voice was heartbreaking.

"Of course, it is. You know you are welcome any time."

Andrew smiled slightly. "I didn't even know where you were until I rang Sofia."

"She's the only one that still talked to me. You were still too young."

"Well, I'm eighteen now. I turned eighteen yesterday."

I chuckled. "So, you did. Happy birthday. How about you alter, and we get out of here. You can come and meet Arley and Flynn. They are my mates, just not officially yet."

Andrew looked up at me with confusion on his face. "I don't even know how that works. But thank you."

"Any time, brother."

Andrew stood and stripped from his clothes. Quickly he altered, and my eyes widened. He wasn't a bear shifter. He was a raccoon. When he changed back, I was still staring at him in shock.

"What? Didn't you know?" he asked with an amused look.

I shook my head. "Andrew, we are all bear shifters, even Mama and Dad."

Andrew nodded. "I know. But Mama's boss is a raccoon shifter."

"Did Dad know that you weren't his?"

"Yeah, he's only known for a couple of years. I was shifted in the backyard with a couple of my friends, and he came home and saw me. He demanded to know why I wasn't a bear shifter. Like I had any idea. I didn't know. That was when he confronted Mama. Beat the living hell out of her. Even when she was shifted, she had wounds on her body. After that, he hated me. He came down harder on me."

It made a lot of sense. If Andrew wasn't Dad's, it made sense why he had Reece beat the hell out of him. It made me hate that man even more.

Chapter Seventeen

Arley

I'd promised Harry and Flynn that I would go over to Harry's home after finishing with the AJE authority. There wasn't a whole lot that was expected from us. We were used as muscle most of the time when there was a raid. But for now, it was more about recon work, and Kade tended to use the Onyx Rebels for that.

I didn't mind. I liked that I got to spend more time at the compound. The only thing that would make spending time at the compound better was if my mates were living with me. My mates. I couldn't wait to be able to say that, and it be the truth.

I pulled into Harry's driveway, and the front door swung open. A teenage boy came bouncing out with wide eyes. His black hair framed his face. And he had an expression of excitement all over him.

"You're one of the Devil's Advocates?" he said.

I laughed and nodded my head. "I am. Who are you?"

"I'm Andrew," he replied, thrusting his hand to shake mine. "I'm Harry's brother."

"Ah," I said, remembering that Harry had mentioned his youngest brother, who wasn't very popular at home. He'd said that he was going to try contacting him. "Well, it's nice to meet you, Andrew. How about we go inside, so I can give Harry a kiss."

"And Flynn?"

I laughed. "And Flynn."

Andrew bounced happily beside me. Looking at the kid, he had to be around eighteen, but his personality was so much younger. It made me wonder if he had some kind of disability or was just a little immature due to his upbringing.

"Hey, baby," I said as I walked into the living room.

Harry was standing in the doorway with a smile on his lips. "As soon as he heard the motorbike, he was out the door in a flash."

I chuckled and leaned forward, pressing a kiss to Harry's lips. Flynn came to stand beside Harry, and I leaned over, kissing him gently on the lips. It was just a brief kiss, and when I looked at Flynn, he had an adorable blush coating his cheeks, but his smile was wantonly sexy.

"Something smells so good in here," I said as I lifted my nose in the air and inhaled.

"That will be our dinner," Andrew called from the kitchen. "I'm making a white wine carbonara with calamari and clams."

"Oh wow, that sounds brilliant," I replied as I entered the kitchen.

Pots were bubbling on the stove, and I watched as Andrew bustled around the kitchen like it was second nature to him.

"Andrew is about to start culinary school in the summer," Flynn said.

"Well, if you can cook like this, your talent would be wasted doing anything else."

Andrew's grin was magnetic. "That's what I'd always tried telling my father."

"Then he was a fool if he didn't see it."

Andrew smiled and nodded his head. His chest puffed with pride. Looking at him, he reminded me a bit of Iver. The tiniest amount of praise, and he thrived on it. I turned back to Harry and Flynn and smiled.

"How was your day?"

"Boring," Harry laughed.

"I helped River go over her dance; now she has it in order."

I groaned. "I think you really need to show me the dance."

Flynn's cheeks tinted pink, and a small giggle fell from his lips.

"Not in front of me, if you don't mind," Andrew said with a laugh.

I snorted and looked over my shoulder. "We will wait for when you are at school."

"That long?" Harry whined.

I barked out a laugh and leaned forward, kissing him gently on the lips. "There will be plenty of time.

"Um, Harry?" Andrew asked. "If I'm in the way of you, just say so. I can find somewhere else to stay."

Harry shook his head firmly. "No. You will never be in the way. I was just teasing Arley. I promise you that I want you here."

Andrew looked like he wasn't wholly convinced but nodded his head. I would have to introduce him to the Devils. Trudy would love to learn to cook from him, and I know that there would be so many members that he would get along with. It might even convince Harry and Flynn to move out to the compound with me.

Chapter Eighteen

Flynn

Andrew went to Harry's spare room to sleep not long after dinner. He was eating dinner, but his eyes were basically hanging out of his head with exhaustion. The poor guy had been running on adrenalin since he was beaten.

"So, did you ring Andrew?" Arley asked as we sat on the couch. I was curled up against Arley's side. Since our playtime the other day, I'd not been able to get close enough to either man. I needed them by my side.

Harry shook his head. "No. He rocked up at the office this morning. His nose was broken, and his eyes were black. I think he had broken ribs too."

Arley hissed. I'd already heard the story, so it didn't have the same effect on me the second time. "Fucking hell. So, you're letting him stay, right?"

Harry nodded. "Absolutely. Unless he wants to go back, there is no way I'm sending him back there."

Arley sighed with relief. "Good. I'd like to take him out to the compound. I reckon he would get along with a few of the guys. We've got a few kids his age."

Harry smiled. "That would be fantastic. I'll ask him."

"I mean, I'd like to take both of you out there. In fact, I'd really like it if you all moved out there with me."

I looked up at Arley and grinned. "You'd really want that?"

Arley chuckled and pressed a kiss to the top of my head. "Of course, I would. I want my mates by my side."

"Well, we aren't mates yet."

Arley shrugged his shoulders. "That's true. And I will never force you to make that decision. But we are only waiting on your say so."

My eyes widened. "Really?"

Arley laughed and nodded his head. "Really."

"Oh. I didn't realize you were waiting for me to make the decision. I just thought that you all wanted to go slow. I guess I knew you were all going slow for my sake, but I didn't know you were literally waiting for me."

"There is no rush. I'm prepared to wait for as long as you need," Harry said.

I looked over at him and smiled. "And if I didn't want to wait anymore?"

"Then you say the word, and I will take you back to that bedroom and make you ours," Arley responded.

I bit into my bottom lip. The thought that Andrew was in the other room floated through my mind. I wasn't sure if it was disrespectful to fuck while he was in the other room. I wasn't sure what to do.

"I want to. Can we be quiet?" I asked.

Arley chuckled. "We can most definitely try. I might have to buy gags."

My eyes widened, but my cock gave a strange jolt. Arley moaned. "Did that turn you on?" he sighed.

I giggled and shrugged my shoulders. "Maybe a little."

Arley chuckled and glanced over at Harry. "Do you want to?"

Harry's head looked like it was about to bounce off with excitement as he nodded. I laughed and stood from the couch, pulling Arley up behind me. I reached out for Harry's hand and tugged, getting him to stand before I led them down the hall to Harry's room. Thankfully, when Harry's house was built; the main bedroom was on the other side of the house from the spare room that Andrew was currently sleeping in. It meant he was less likely to hear our activities.

No sooner had the door closed on Harry's bedroom did I have my clothes off. Arley and Harry moaned simultaneously as they took me in. I had slight nerves floating around me, but my unicorn pushed against me. I wasn't scared that they would hurt me. I loved them both. I needed them both.

Arley slipped Harry's shirt off over his head, and I moaned as his chest covered in brown hair was revealed. When Arley unzipped Harry's pants, they fell to his ankles, revealing his beautiful body. I fell to my knees in front of Harry and ran my nose along the inside of his thigh. Harry moaned and ran his fingers down over my hair. Licking up along his shaft, I swirled my tongue around the head of his cock before opening my lips and sucking him to the back of my throat.

"Fuck, that feels so fucking good," he moaned as I bobbed my head up and down. I rolled his balls gently in my hand and moved my fingers of my other hand around over his ass, and between his cheeks, I fingered his hole.

Harry widened his legs with a moan to give me better access to his hole. I reached between my legs, coating my fingers in the slick dripping from me and bringing them back to his ass. Harry groaned as I penetrated him and pressed on his prostate. His cock kicked in my mouth, and a spray of precum fell from his slit, coating my tongue in its salty taste.

Chapter Nineteen

Arley

I wanted to rip Flynn off the couch and carry him to the bedroom like a caveman when he said he wanted to mate with us. I didn't realize just how much my alpha wanted him. I'd wished to have no one more than I wished to have Flynn and Harry.

Watching Flynn on his knees finger fucking Harry while he sucked his cock was out of this world. For the first time in my life since leaving those pedophiles behind, I thought I might have found the men that I would actually bottom for.

Flynn stood and glanced over at me. I'd taken my clothes off and stood naked in front of them with a smile on my lips.

"I want to ride you," he said to me with a slight smile on his lips.

I nodded my head. I walked wordlessly towards Harry's bed and laid down on my back.

"Harry, I want you to ride my face. I want you nice and wet. I'm going to stretch you because I will fuck you too," I directed.

Harry and Flynn moaned, and I knew my suggestion was taken well. Flynn moved up the bed and crawled across my lap.

"We stop anytime you want," I reassured him.

"I trust you," he replied with a smile.

Those three words meant more to me than if he had told me he loved me. Hearing him say that he trusted me was everything.

Flynn took my cock with one hand and slowly lowered himself onto it. I groaned as my cock pushed through the tight ring of muscles into his warm channel. The slick that leaked out of him lubricated the way.

Flynn gasped, and his eyes rolled as he slowly rocked back against me. "That feels so good," he whispered.

Harry moved onto the bed, and I glanced up at him. "Straddle my face," I directed.

Harry bit into his bottom lip as he nodded his head. Slowly he lifted his leg over my face and kneeled on either side of my head. I took hold of his hips and lowered him down, flicking my tongue over his hole. I took great delight in the moan that fell from his lips.

I started to stroke up and down his shaft with my other hand. It didn't take long before Harry ground against my tongue. I repeatedly speared his prostate, alternating between my tongue and fingers to stretch out his pleasure.

Flynn bounced on my cock, and our moans and skin slapping echoed throughout the room. I gave a brief thought to Andrew, but at the moment, there was nothing I could do, well, there was, but I just didn't care enough to keep my mates quiet.

My alpha was desperate to give our mates their mating mark. Flynn and Harry must have felt the same way as Flynn climbed off my body when Harry did.

Flynn looked down at me and smiled. "I need Harry's knot, and I need to watch you fuck him simultaneously."

I nodded my head. Flynn moved onto his back on the bed and lifted his legs. His hole was stretched from my cock, and slick glistened in the room's light.

Harry moved to hover over Flynn, moaning as he guided his cock deep inside him. I moved to the back of Harry and ran my cock up and down his crease. Harry rolled his hips, encouraging me to penetrate him. I pushed slowly inside him with a moan.

My thrusts guided Harry's, and soon we were all moaning. The feeling of power in the room was overwhelming, and I knew that we weren't far. My fangs elongated, and I stared down at Flynn, watching me. He moved slightly so that his chest was bared to me. I nodded my head at the silent invitation. Moving forward with a roar, I bit into Flynn's chest. His blood coated my tongue and sent me over the edge of pleasure.

The minute I felt his return bite, I orgasmed once more. I couldn't take it any longer and leaned forward, biting into Harry's shoulder. Harry moaned loudly, and I watched as he bit into Flynn on the opposite of his chest. Flynn cried out, and his eyes rolled as he answered Harry's bite.

"Fuck yes," Harry roared as he turned his head as much as possible and bit into my bicep, the only part he could get to.

Slowly, I came down from the stratosphere and pulled out of Harry, watching in delight as cum dribbled from his used hole. I rolled onto my back beside Flynn and reached out for his hand. Linking my fingers with his.

"I love you both," Flynn said with a slight whisper.

I turned to look at him and Harry. "I love you both too."

Harry grinned. "I love you both as well," he answered.

After so long waiting, dancing around one another, wondering if this would ever happen, I had my mates. My two mates. I had to be the luckiest vampire on earth.

Chapter Twenty

Harry

Thankfully Andrew didn't mention that he heard us mating when he'd gotten up the following day. He commented on how much happier I looked now that I was mated. I had to admit I was more optimistic. It had been three weeks, and so much had changed for me in just those three weeks.

We went to the Devil's Advocates compound the day after our mating. Andrew rode on the back of Arley's bike, which he loved. The smile on his face told me everything. Arley introduced him to many people, including a young guy named Walker, a prospect for the Devil's and the same age as Andrew.

By the way that Andrew blushed and reacted to Walker to the way they snuck off, I wasn't in the least bit surprised when Andrew came back later that night with a mate mark. I was thrilled for him. It was ironic that had Dad's goon not beaten Andrew, sending him running to me, then he would never have met Walker. Mother fate sure did have exciting timing.

I was worried that being mated would mean that Andrew wouldn't go to culinary school. But apparently, he and Walker had talked a lot first about it, and they had a plan. I was really happy for him. Of course, I couldn't wait to find out if Flynn was pregnant.

Flynn loved being at the Devil's Advocates compound because he was close to Dylan. First, I thought, I might feel jealous when I saw him and Dylan together, knowing they'd played together. Even though they hadn't actually touched. But there was no jealousy there. I could see that Dylan was entirely in love with Jai, and there was no desire to take my man.

Arley asked whether we would be willing to move to the compound. It wasn't even a difficult decision to make. I wanted to be wherever my mates were. Flynn felt the same way. So here we were three weeks later, moving into a new house on the compound. The home that Arley had been living in was a small one-bedroom apartment for the unmated alphas. But now we were moving into a large house.

A carpenter in the area, Maddox, had designed our bed for us to easily fit the three of us. A couple of the guys related to Bacchus, the president's mate, were excited to design the nursery if Flynn was pregnant. Of course, we still had to take a pregnancy test.

I was a little nervous about how Flynn would react if he was pregnant. After the loss of Albany, I was worried that he wouldn't want any more children. But when we'd spoken about it, he said he would welcome a little one.

Arley and I had organized some of the photos that Flynn had of Albany to be blown up and placed on a canvas to hang in the house. It was the only decoration piece on the wall, but they were the most important in my mind. Flynn's happy tears had told me that we did the right thing this morning when he came in and saw them.

"What do you think?" I asked Flynn as I stood in the living room with my arm around him.

"I think it's beautiful. I'm happy," he said with a bright smile.

"Me too," I replied with a kiss on his head.

Even though it had been a great three weeks of being mated, it was also hectic. Flynn had undergone many tests to discover why he couldn't shift, when we thought we'd had them over and done with, Dr. Rankin sent him for more. We were due to go back to the doctors during the week to get the results, and I knew that he was nervous. If I was truthful, I would be able to say that I was terrified.

"Can you see yourself living here for the rest of your life?" I asked.

Flynn turned to me with a bright smile and bounced his head up and down. "Most definitely. I can also see us having children here. They would have all their friends right by their side."

My grin must have been enormous. The fact that he was so open about having children thrilled me.

"Hey guys, I expected Arley to be here," a girl said. Her hair was cropped short, and she had so much muscle that if it hadn't been because she had boobs and wore a dress, I might not have realized she was a girl.

"He's just gone to pick up some things with Anghus and Zion. I'm Harry, and this is Flynn; we are Arley's mates," I introduced.

"Well, it's great to meet you both. I'm Harper."

"Oh, Harper. Arley told us about you. And you are Walker's sister. Andrew is my brother," I said.

Harper grinned. "That's awesome. It's good to meet you. I only dropped by to congratulate him on finally finding his mates, but I'm glad I met you both."

"You too."

Harper smiled and turned, leaving the house. "God, that training she did, turned her into a machine," Flynn said with wide eyes.

I nodded my head. "Yeah, I wouldn't want to meet her in a dark alley."

"Me neither," Flynn replied with a giggle.

Chapter Twenty-One

Flynn

"Flynn, come on in," Dr. Rankin called.

I stood with Harry and Arley by my side. I'd been a nervous wreck last night and this morning at the thought of coming to the doctors. The idea of it was terrifying. I didn't want to be told the bad news.

"Hello Flynn, I see you've brought your mates; it's nice to see you both," Dr. Rankin said as he directed us into his office.

I took a seat with Harry and Arley on either side of me. Dr. Rankin sat down and turned his computer screen so we could see it.

"Alright, this is your brain. And to me, it looks completely normal. There are no signs of any tumors or abnormalities, which is good. However, it doesn't tell us why you are unable to shift. All of your blood tests returned completely normal, and the full-body scan. Oh well, except one thing."

"What's that?" I asked with a frown, feeling my heart leap into my chest.

"You're pregnant." I barked out a laugh with surprise and grinned, turning to face Harry and Arley, who looked equally excited. Dr. Rankin chuckled. "Thought you might like that news. You will need another ultrasound to check on the baby's condition and growth, but all babies looked good and in the right place."

"Wait, babies?" Harry said with surprise.

"Yep. You are pregnant with triplets."

"Holy shit," Arley whispered.

Dr. Rankin chuckled again. "You will need to be checked more closely than the average pregnancy because you're carrying multiples. Plus, with the history, you have with your daughter. Not that SIDs are necessarily a pregnancy issue. However, studies just recently come out that showed there could be a genetic factor with SIDs."

I gasped. "So, they could tell whether one of my children is likely to have it?"

"Not just yet, but they are most definitely on the road to discovery."

"That's great news," Harry said from beside me.

Dr. Rankin nodded his head. "However, we still have a problem of why you can't shift. Can you tell me more about your family history?"

I shrugged my shoulders. "I'm afraid I don't know a lot. My mother was a unicorn, but I didn't know who my father was. I don't know if Mama could shift or not. She was an alcoholic and drug addict, so I don't even know if she is still alive."

Dr. Rankin nodded his head. "I'm sorry you went through that. That's okay. I'm leaning towards thinking this is a genetic thing. I've spoken to a few of my colleagues about the issue. I've discovered that in some supernatural/human pairings, it changes the DNA enough that the resulting child is born supernatural. However, they might not have all of the abilities a supernatural does. So, in your case, your father could be human, and therefore you've been unable to shift."

My eyes widened. I hadn't even thought that was possible. But I supposed nothing was stopping a human from creating a child with a supernatural. It wasn't like you had to be mated to produce a child.

"I never even thought about my father potentially being a human."

Dr. Rankin smiled. "We can do DNA testing to find out. Unless he is in the DNA database, it won't tell us who your father is. But what it will do is tell us whether or not he was human or supernatural. It will also tell us what kind of supernatural he was if he was."

I nodded my head. "That would be good. I can imagine it is important information I might need to know for when the babies are born."

Dr. Rankin nodded. "Yes, quite right." He turned and opened a drawer pulling out a kit. "All it takes is a swab from your mouth, and we should have the results in around about a month. I would like them back sooner, but unfortunately, it does take that long due to the backup."

"That's okay," I replied as I opened my mouth so that Dr. Rankin could swab the inside of my cheeks.

He placed the swab in a tube and sealed it in a plastic bag. "When that comes back, I'll give you a ring, and we will book another appointment for you to come back in. In the meantime, I'm going to set up a referral for you to get an ultrasound, so we can start checking the babies."

"Thank you so much," I replied. I felt like the world had lifted off my shoulders. There wasn't anything seemingly wrong with me, and it could have just been the way I was conceived that was the cause of my inability to shift. And to boot, I was about to have three children. I wish that Albany was here to meet her little brothers or sisters, but either way, it was time to start living and enjoying life again. I had my mates, and I was about to have my children. Life was great.

***

The month went by so quickly. The ultrasound had shown that I had three babies growing inside me. We'd decided to keep the genders a secret, this way, it would be a surprise when they were born. I was excited. My belly was popping out, and I couldn't wait to be able to hold my children in my arms. Thankfully, I lavished every part of the pregnancy, not the morning sickness, but that moved on quickly.

Dr. Rankin rang and made an appointment to see me, so Harry, Arley, and I sat back in his office waiting for the news of my DNA test.

"Well, I got the results yesterday from your DNA test, as I suspected, your father was human. Which would explain why you cannot shift," Dr. Rankin explained.

"Will that affect the children? If they are born shifters?" Harry asked.

"Possibly, it will be something we have to wait and see. They might have the same problem, but it could only affect Flynn. At this stage, we just can't tell until the babies are born."

"But otherwise, they would be completely healthy?" Arley asked.

Dr. Rankin smiled and nodded his head. "Absolutely. The scans you've had and the checkups show there isn't anything unordinary with the babies."

"Was my father in the DNA system?" I asked out of curiosity.

"No. However, we do have a family line for him. The problem is that I'm not allowed to give that information out. You can go through one of the ancestry DNA groups, and you will be able to connect through that," Dr. Rankin replied with a smile.

I shook my head. "No need. I'm not interested; I was just a little curious. But if he never bothered seeing me all that time, there was no point in getting to know him."

Dr. Rankin smiled and nodded his head. "That is your decision to make. But the information is out there should you ever want it."

I had been thinking about whether that was something I would want to know over the last month. But in the end, I knew it didn't matter. I wasn't my father. Nor was I, my mother. If he hadn't bothered to be there for me as a child and as I grew, then there was nothing I wanted from him as an adult.

Epilogue

Arley

I sat in awe, looking down at my three children. Three daughters. And three little vampires. I couldn't believe it. They were the most beautiful little girls I'd ever laid eyes on. They all had my dark hair and red eyes, with Flynn's nose and lips. I had felt a pinch of pain when I realized that I'd been the girls' biological father.

However, when Harry and I talked about it, he informed me that he couldn't be happier. They were his daughters, too, regardless of whether he shared DNA or not. It was perfect. I was in love; I had my two mates and three little girls.

Of course, when we brought them home, everyone had been quick to come and visit, making sure that Flynn was coping well after the caesarian. Not being able to shift it meant that he had to heal slowly. However, everyone was happy to bring food and help around the house until he could move more quickly.

"I'm so happy for you, man," Zion said as he held one of the girls.

"Alright, alright, you have to tell us their names," Larissa laughed.

We had been having all sorts of trouble trying to decide on names. We'd decided to wait until they were born to see what their names were, but we still were struggling with ideas.

"Do you want some help, Uncle Arley?" Iver asked.

I chuckled and glanced at Flynn, who grinned. "Finally, someone who can tell us."

Iver giggled. "This one," he said, pointing to the little girl in Zion's arms. "Is Amaia. And that one," he pointed to the little girl that Harry was holding. "Is Kora and finally this one," he said to the little one in my arms. "She is Darcey."

I grinned and looked down at my daughter. "Oh, my stars, she smiled," Harry gasped at the same time that I watched Darcey grin.

"Amaia did too," Zion said with amazement.

"So did Darcey. Iver you've done it again," I chuckled.

Iver's face lit up, and he moved to each girl before putting a small kiss on their cheeks and whispering something in each of their ears that sounded like a blessing. But really, it was me that was blessed. I had my mates, and I had my daughters. There was no way that life could get any better.

Suddenly Andrew came rushing into the living room, his eyes were wide, and he had fear on his face. Harry looked up with concern. "Andrew, what's wrong?"

"Harry. They've arrested Mama and Dad."

Harry gasped, and his eyes widened. "For what?"

Andrew shook his head. "I don't know for sure, but Sofia just rang. She's been trying to ring you, but your phone is off."

Harry nodded his head. "I forgot to turn it on once we left the hospital."

Andrew was pacing back and forth, chewing on his thumbnail while Harry handed Kora to Flynn. He went to where he'd left his phone and turned it back on. Bings sounded through the phone as the messages from his sister pinged through.

Harry ignored them all and pressed the phone to his ear. "Sofia? Sorry, I forgot to turn my phone on again once we left the hospital."

I couldn't hear Sofia's response, but Harry's frown deepened. "Alright. I'll call you later." Ending the call, he glanced around the room. "Apparently, Dad has been financing Ettore."

"What the fuck?" I said with a gasp.

"That bastard," Andrew spat while Walker looked furious.

"Jesus," Zion said with a shake of his head.

"I'm so sorry, guys," Larissa said with a sigh just as Anghus and Bacchus came into the living room.

"Ah, I see you guys have heard," Anghus said.

We nodded our heads simultaneously. "How did this happen?" Andrew asked Bacchus.

"The vampire team has been watching your father for some time. Apparently, an anonymous tip-off a few weeks ago told the AJE authority that Jonathon and Judith were working for Ettore. They were doing research on the side, and Jonathon had been funding it," Bacchus explained. "Kade and the team finally got the evidence they needed to make the arrest early this morning."

"Christ," I said with a shake of my head. "So, he has been part of helping these super alphas being built?"

Bacchus nodded. "It seems that way. I'm sorry to do this to you guys, but I've been asked to bring the inner crew of the Devil's in along with the Onyx Rebels to help sort through the evidence."

"Not you, Arley, spend time with your babies. Walker can step into your role," Anghus said.

Walker's head spun to look at the president with wide eyes. "You mean it?" he asked.

Anghus smiled and nodded his head. "You've proved yourself."

The smile that lit up Walker's face was spectacular. I was just glad that I got to stay home and spend time with my girls and my mates. Zion passed Amaia over to Larissa with a chuckle.

"Well, sweet girl, I've enjoyed the cuddles, but duty calls," Zion said before placing a small kiss on Amaia's head. He went around to each girl and kissed their heads before leaving the house with Walker, Anghus, and Bacchus.

"Do you think he will go to jail?" Andrew asked.

"I guess it depends on their evidence against him," I replied.

Andrew nodded his head. "No doubt he will have Jonathon as his representation."

Harry nodded his head. I knew that Harry's older brother was a lawyer, but I didn't know how good he was. But it might not matter. If they had enough evidence to convict him, it might not matter who represented him. I was curious as to who the tip-off had been. Flynn was obviously thinking the same thing.

"Do you think your Mama tipped them off?" he glanced between Harry and Andrew.

Andrew's eyes widened. "Maybe. I never thought of that. I always wondered why she never left him. But maybe this was why? Maybe she was stuck and just needed to get enough evidence to sink him."

"But if that's the case, she has to sink herself too," Harry said.

"What's that saying? If you lie with dogs, you're gonna get fleas," Andrew responded.

Harry sighed and nodded his head. I guess only time was going to tell what would happen. I was glad to have another of Ettore's goons off the street. I was curious and part of me kind of wanted to go into the AJE authority to see what was being done. But my heart was definitely more than happy to remain home with my mates and my daughters. Now they were my main priority. Everything else would have to wait.

Ettore would get his, and I hoped that I would still be alive to watch my daughters grow up to help to kick his ass.

"I wonder what their powers are?" Larissa said as she broke into my thoughts.

"They can communicate telepathically," Iver responded. "They are already having silent conversations with one another. But as they get older, they will be able to communicate with anyone they meet."

My eyes widened and I stared down at Darcey who smiled back up at me as if to say that what Iver said was the truth.

"I hope they are able to turn that off if they want a break," Harry mumbled.

Iver smiled and nodded his head. "As they get older, they will learn how to switch it on and off. But there will come a day that they won't speak much verbally instead all of their communication will be done through their minds."

I shook my head in astonishment. My daughters were amazing. I couldn't believe that the creator had blessed me so much. Not only did I have the most amazing mates, I'd adopted a fantastic family and now I had three daughters of my own that would be integral in bringing down the evil reign of Ettore. It was perfect. Absolutely perfect.

The End.

Don't miss out!

Visit the website below and you can sign up to receive emails whenever S L Davies publishes a new book. There's no charge and no obligation.

https://books2read.com/r/B-A-NZRR-RJEBC

BOOKS 2 READ

Connecting independent readers to independent writers.

Also by S L Davies

Breeding Facility
Memphis
Bacchus
Coltrane
Pax
Raiden
Nash

Devil's Advocates
Lynx
Israel
Jai
Jasper
Arley
Zion
Oakland

KINK
Freya
Tanquil

Obsidian Mechanics
Donte

Onyx Rebels
Onyx Rebels Prologue
Hawke

Rigby Brothers
Asher

Schiavu
Schiavu

Standalone
Sisters Revenge
Killer Love
Soldiers At War
Second Chances
Bunny
Caged

Watch for more at https://www.amazon.com/~/e/B0832T8F7Z.

About the Author

S L Davies is an Australian Author living in Country, Victoria. She is inspired by the world around her.

Read more at https://www.amazon.com/~/e/B0832T8F7Z.